MARVEL STUDIOS

CAPTAIN AMERICA™

THE FIRST AVENGER

THE GREAT ESCAPE

Adapted by
Elizabeth Rudnick

Based on the Motion Picture Screenplay by
Christopher Markus & Stephen McFeely

MARVEL

NEW YORK

Published by Marvel Press, an imprint of Disney Book Group. No part of this book may
be reproduced or transmitted in any form or by any means, electronic or mechanical,
including photocopying, recording, or by any information storage and retrieval system,
without written permission from the publisher. For information address Marvel Press, 114
Fifth Avenue, New York, New York 10011-5690.

Printed in the United States of America

First Edition

1 3 5 7 9 10 8 6 4 2

J689-1817-1-11121

ISBN 978-1-4231-4314-7

Not very long ago, Steve Rogers was just an
ordinary man. All he wanted was to be a soldier
in the army and help win the war.

And then one day, his wish came true.

Steve was chosen to take part in a very
important experiment, Project: Rebirth. He was
given a special serum that transformed him from
a thin, frail man into a Super-Soldier.

HE BECAME CAPTAIN AMERICA!

Colonel Phillips, who helped train Steve for Project: Rebirth, was not happy. He had gotten only one soldier out of the experiment before a spy destroyed the lab. Phillips wanted to use Steve to duplicate the process and make more Super-Soldiers, but Senator Brandt didn't agree.

"You don't take a soldier, a symbol, like this and hide him in a lab," Brandt said. He had much bigger plans for Captain America.

Backstage in a small theater, Steve was getting
ready for his first job as America's newest hero.
Then a line of dancing girls took to the stage.

"*He's the star-spangled man with the star-
spangled plan. He's Captain America,*" the girls sang.

With a gulp, Steve stepped out and squinted
against the glare of the spotlight.

"Hello . . . folks," he read, glancing at the cue
card hidden in his shield. "Who is ready to sock evil
in the jaw?"

There were a few halfhearted cheers.

This was not going well.

But Steve wasn't going to give up. He needed to encourage people to fight, so he kept performing.

And slowly, from one town to another, people started coming to see Captain America.

Each city brought a bigger stage and more people. By the time he returned to New York, Steve was a celebrity. He hadn't actually fought in the war, but that didn't seem to matter.

Captain America was a symbol of American power.

Then Captain America was sent to Italy, five miles from the front lines.

This time, instead of cheers, Steve was met with boos.

A few dozen GIs sat in the audience, glaring at him.

Steve looked down at his spotless uniform and shiny boots and then out at the men who'd been

fighting. Their uniforms were dirty, and their boots were scuffed. He gulped and then went on, "I'm going to need a volunteer."

"I already volunteered," one of the soldiers shouted. "How do you think I got here?"

The crowd shouted in agreement. Another man called out, "Bring back the dancing girls!"

A short while later, Steve sat in the now-empty theater. What had he been thinking? He wasn't a hero. He was a fool.

The sound of footsteps made him look up. Peggy Carter, the British agent who had helped pick Steve for the experiment, was walking toward him.

Peggy knew Steve was upset. And she had more bad news. "We got word that HYDRA was moving a

force through Azzano," Peggy said. Steve tensed.
HYDRA was an evil group intent on destroying
the world.

Peggy continued. "Two hundred men went in,
and less than fifty came back. Your adoring crowd
tonight contained all that's left of the 107th."

Steve sat up. His best friend, Bucky Barnes,
was in the 107th!

"I want to see the casualty list," Steve demanded, barging into Colonel Phillips's tent. "I don't need the whole list," Steve went on. "Just one name— Sergeant James Barnes, from the 107th."

Colonel Phillips picked up the large stack of papers in front of him and began to leaf through it. "The name does sound familiar . . . " He paused over one sheet. Then he looked up. "I'm sorry."

Bucky had been captured.

Steve turned and raced out of the room. He was going after Bucky!

Agent Peggy Carter went to the only man that could help Steve with his plan—millionaire industrialist Howard Stark. Stark helped Steve "borrow" a plane from the U.S. Army for the rescue mission.

Night had fallen over the Italian countryside. In the camp, things were quiet. Suddenly, the sound of a plane engine roared.

Inside a large jet, Steve readied his parachute while Peggy gave him a quick briefing.

"The HYDRA camp contains a factory of some kind," she explained.

"We should be able to drop you right on the doorstep," Stark added.

Suddenly, the sound of gunfire filled the air. They were being shot at!

Steve opened the side door and prepared to jump.

"Once I'm clear, turn this thing around and get out of here," Steve commanded.

"You can't give me orders!" Peggy shouted back.

Steve turned and gave her one last smile. "Yes I can," he said. "I'm Captain America."

Then he jumped.

The wind rushed by as Steve plummeted toward the ground. Below, a dense forest spread out in all directions. Hidden somewhere inside was the HYDRA factory—and Bucky.

Steve quickly and quietly made his way to the main gates of the compound.

Smoke billowed out of the factories. Barbed wire sat atop a high fence. HYDRA soldiers patrolled the perimeter. Catching sight of an approaching truck, Steve stepped forward, and then, when no one was looking, he jumped in the back.

A moment later, the truck rolled through the gates. He was in!

Now all he had to do was find Bucky, free him and the rest of the captured men, and escape from the enemy compound. It was an impossible mission for Steve Rogers—but not for Captain America!

Steve looked around and saw a group of prisoners being led into a building. Following them, he found dozens of cages full of captured men.

With one swift move, Steve knocked out the guard and grabbed his keys. Then, before anyone could sound an alarm, he released the men.

But Bucky wasn't with them.

"Are there any more?" Steve asked.

"The isolation ward," a soldier answered. "On the factory floor."

With the others freed, Steve made his way
to the factory, where he saw dozens of HYDRA
agents hard at work. Steve then noticed bombs
and crates full of ammunition. There were also
strange cartridges that glowed blue.

Steve silently made his way past the guards and down a long corridor and snuck into a large holding cell. Inside, a huge iron cage sat atop a rusty drain. Steve could make out the shadow of a prisoner.

The prisoner heard someone approach and immediately spoke. "The only thing you HYDRA bums will get from me is my name, rank, and serial number. Barnes, James Buchanan—"

Steve couldn't believe it—he had found Bucky!

Racing over, Steve smashed the lock with his shield and freed his friend.

"What happened to you?" Bucky asked, amazed at Steve's new strength.

"I joined the army," Steve said with a smile.

Just then, the HYDRA soldiers burst onto the
scene. They were determined to capture the intruder.
Suddenly, the air filled with the sound of

explosions. Steve and Bucky knew that they had
to get out of there—and fast!

Steve and Bucky ran through the hallways of the factory, taking out every HYDRA foot soldier in their path. They still had a long way to go, and there were many dangers ahead. But with Bucky safe and by his side, Steve knew he would make it. Once they escaped, he'd come back to deal with the rest of HYDRA.

But then an explosion rocked the compound, filling it with smoke.

There was no sign of Steve, Bucky, or the men of the 107th!

Back at the base, Peggy sat, concerned. She was sure that Steve had been killed in action.

But just then, she heard a commotion outside. The soldiers were clapping and cheering.

Peggy rushed out to see Steve Rogers and the men of the 107th walking back to the base. They were bruised and beaten, but they were alive. It was a great escape.

Steve smiled at Peggy. Project: Rebirth had been a success. He had finally become a real hero—and had truly earned his name and rank. He really was America's first Super-Soldier.

HE WAS CAPTAIN AMERICA!